A Child's Book of Miracles

by
Sister Mary Kathleen Glavich, S.N.D.

This book belongs to

St. Michael's Montessori Preschool
9-94

Loyola University Press
Chicago 60657

Nihil Obstat: Sister Donna Marie Brodesca, O.S.U., D.Min.
                 Censor Deputatus
Imprimatur: The Most Reverend Anthony M. Pilla, D.D., M.A.
                 Bishop of Cleveland
Given at Cleveland, Ohio, on 7 February 1994.

The Nihil Obstat and Imprimatur are official declarations that a book or pamphlet is free of doctrinal or moral error. No implication is contained therein that those who have granted the Nihil Obstat and Imprimatur agree with the contents, opinions, or statements expressed.

Glavich, Mary Kathleen.
    A child's book of miracles/Mary Kathleen Glavich.
        p. cm.
    Contents: Wine for a wedding—Jesus stops a storm—Peter's mother-in-law—A leper with faith—The man who came through the roof—Jesus frees a crazy man—The widow's son—Walking across water—A deaf man hears—The soldier's servant—Bartimaeus, the blind beggar—Lazarus lives again.
    ISBN 0-8294-0802-9 $2.50
    1. Jesus Christ—Miracles—Juvenile literature.
    [1. Jesus Christ—Miracles. 2. Miracles. 3. Bible stories—N.T.] I. Title.
BT366.G63   1994
226.7'09505—dc20

94-2378
CIP
AC

Illustrations and cover art by Lydia Halverson.

ISBN 0-8294-0802-9   01 00 99 98 97 96 95 94   5 4 3 2 1

Contents

Wine for a Wedding

Based on John 2:1–11

Jesus, his mother Mary, and his friends were at a wedding in the town of Cana. The guests were eating and drinking, talking and laughing. Then Mary saw the servers pouring the last of the wine. There was no more wine, and the party was not over yet! The bride and groom and their families would feel bad.

Mary went to Jesus and said, "They have no wine."

At first Jesus said, "Why should I worry about that? My time has not yet come."

But Mary knew her Son would help. She said to the servers, "Do whatever he tells you."

In the room stood six large stone water jars. Jesus told the servers, "Fill these jars with water." The servers filled the six jars to the top. Then Jesus said, "Take some now to the man in charge." The servers did this.

The water was changed into wine. The man in charge didn't know where the wine had come from. When he tasted it, he called the bridegroom over and said, "Usually people serve the best wine first and then the poorer wine. You have kept the best wine until now."

This was Jesus' first miracle.

❖ Thank Jesus for a gift he has given you.

Jesus Stops a Storm

Based on Mark 4:35–41

Jesus was teaching a crowd of people by the sea. At the
end of the day, he said to his friends, "Let's go across to the
other side." They got into a boat. Jesus rested his head
on a cushion in the back of the boat and fell asleep.

Suddenly a terrible storm came—with thunder,
lightning, and strong winds. Huge waves crashed
onto the boat, filling it with water.

3

The apostles woke up Jesus. They shouted, "Lord, save us. Don't you care that we're drowning?"

Jesus got up and said to the wind and the sea, "Calm down. Be still." Just like that, everything was perfectly still.

Then Jesus asked his friends, "Why are you afraid? Don't you have faith?"

The apostles were surprised at what had happened. They asked one another, "Who is this? Even the wind and the sea obey him."

❖ Tell Jesus that you know he is with you when you are afraid of something.

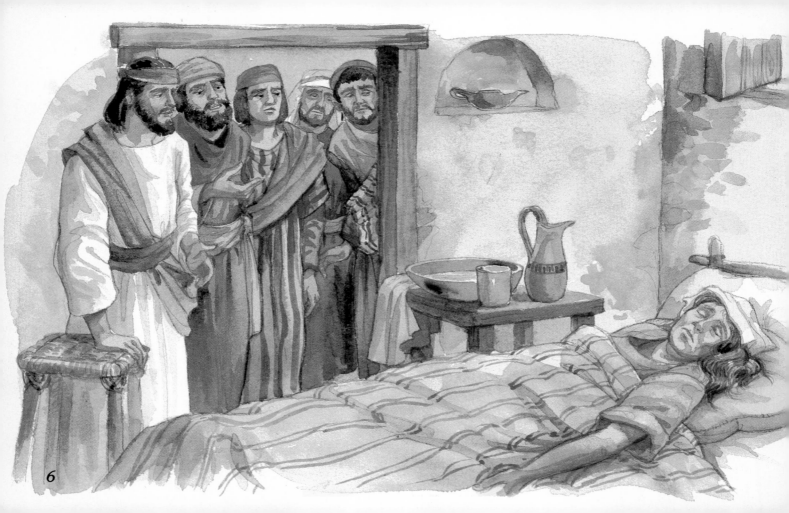

6

Peter's Mother-in-Law

Based on Mark 1:29–31

It was the Lord's Day. Jesus prayed and taught in the Jewish building of worship. Afterwards he walked with James and John to the house where Peter and Andrew lived.

As soon as Jesus entered the house, Peter and Andrew told him that Peter's mother-in-law was very sick. She was in bed with a high fever. The two brothers asked Jesus to do something for her.

Jesus went over to the sick woman. He took her by the hand and helped her up. Right away the fever left her. She began to serve Jesus and the others something to eat.

❖   Ask Jesus to help a sick person you know.

7

A Leper with Faith

Based on Mark 1:40–45

In Jesus' time the awful disease called leprosy was common. Leprosy was so catching that lepers had to live in a special place. Everyone stayed away from them.

One day a man with leprosy came to Jesus and knelt on the ground before him. He said, "Lord, if you want to, you can cure me."

Jesus felt very sorry for the man. Without fear, Jesus stretched out his hand and touched him, saying, "Of course I want to. Be healed."

At Jesus' touch and words, the leprosy went away.

Then Jesus told the man to go show himself to the town leaders. They would see and tell others that he was in good health again. The man left, and he told everyone the story of what Jesus had done for him.

❖ Talk to Jesus about something you would like him to do for you.

9

10

The Man Who Came through the Roof

Based on Mark 2:1–12

When Jesus came back to his town, people heard that he was home and went to listen to him talk about God. People filled the house and stood outside the door. Not one more person could fit inside.

Then a group brought their sick friend to the house. The man wasn't able to move his body at all. Four of his friends carried him on a mat. Because of the crowd, they couldn't get near Jesus. The men climbed up to the flat roof of the house and made a hole in it above Jesus. Then they carefully lowered their friend on the mat.

Jesus saw how much they believed in him. He said to the sick man, "Courage, child, your sins are forgiven."

Some of the town leaders there were thinking, "Who does he think he is? Only God can forgive sins."

Jesus read their minds. He asked, "Which is easier to say to the man, 'Your sins are forgiven,' or, 'Rise, pick up your mat, and walk'? I'm healing this man to show you that I can forgive sins too."

11

Jesus then said to the man on the mat, "I say to you, rise, pick up your mat, and go home." The man rose, picked up his mat, and walked away through the crowd.

Everyone praised God and said, "What wonderful things we have seen today."

❖ Ask Jesus to make you a good friend to others.

Jesus Frees a Crazy Man

Based on Luke 8:26–39

Once there was a man who was crazy and dangerous. People said there was an evil spirit in him. They tried to chain him down, but he always broke the chains. He did not wear clothes or live in a house. Instead he stayed in a cemetery. There night and day he ran among the tombs, howling and hurting himself with stones.

13

14

One day Jesus crossed the sea and came to the land where the crazy man lived. When Jesus got out of the boat, the man ran to him and fell down before him. Jesus said, "Evil spirit, come out of the man." The man shouted, "Jesus, Son of God, do not hurt me."

Jesus asked, "What is your name?"

The man answered, "I have more names than you can count," because there was a great number of evil spirits in him.

Many pigs were feeding on the hillside. The evil spirits begged, "Do not drive us away to hell. Send us into the pigs."

So Jesus let the evil spirits leave the man and go into the pigs. The pigs rushed down a cliff into the sea and were drowned. The men who took care of the pigs ran away. They told everyone what had happened.

People came to see for themselves. They saw Jesus with the crazy man sitting at his feet, dressed and back to normal. The people were afraid and begged Jesus to leave. When Jesus got into the boat, the cured man asked to go with him. But Jesus told him, "Go home to your family and tell them all that the Lord has done for you."

❖   Ask Jesus to keep you from evil.

15

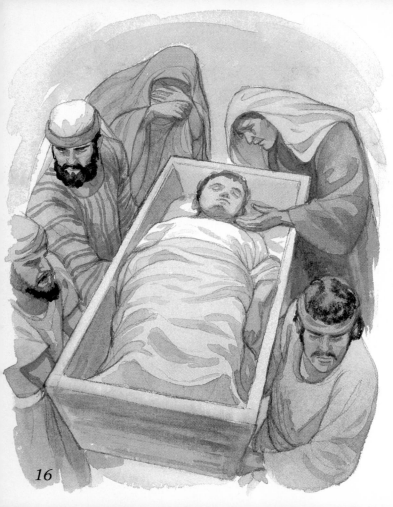

The Widow's Son

Based on Luke 7:11–17

Jesus and his friends went to the city Nain. A large crowd came too. When the group reached Nain, they saw many people coming out of the city. Some of them were carrying a dead man. His mother walked near the coffin, crying. Her husband had died earlier, and now her only son was dead too.

When Jesus saw the mother, he felt sorry for her. "Don't cry," he said.

Jesus stepped up and touched the coffin. The men carrying it stopped. Then Jesus said, "Young man, I tell you, get up."

The dead man sat up and started talking. Jesus handed him to his mother. Everyone was afraid. Then they gave glory to God.

❖ If you know people who have died, ask Jesus to bless them and their families.

17

Walking across Water

Based on Matthew 14:22–33

One day Jesus told the apostles to get into the boat and cross the lake. He said he would come later. After his friends left, Jesus went up on a mountain to pray by himself.

By evening the boat was far out on the lake. A strong wind blew, and waves tossed the boat on the sea. The apostles were tired of rowing. Late at night they saw someone walking toward them on the sea. It was Jesus, but they didn't know it. "It's a ghost," they said, and they yelled in fear.

Jesus called to them, "Have courage. It is I. Don't be afraid."

Peter said, "Lord, if it is you, tell me to come to you on the water."

"Come," Jesus answered.

So Peter climbed out of the boat and began to walk on top of the water toward Jesus. Peter was all right until he thought about the strong wind. Then he became afraid and began to sink. He cried out, "Lord, save me!"

At once Jesus reached out and caught him. "O, you of little faith," Jesus said to Peter, "why don't you trust me?"

Then Jesus and Peter walked to the boat and got in. The wind stopped. The others in the boat bowed down to Jesus. They said, "Truly you are the Son of God."

❖ Ask Jesus to give you a strong trust in him.

20

A Deaf Man Hears

Based on Mark 7:31–37

One day people brought a deaf man to Jesus. The man couldn't speak well either. The people begged Jesus to lay his hand on the man to cure him.

Jesus took the man a little way from the crowd. He put his finger in the man's ears and touched the man's tongue with spittle. Then Jesus looked up to heaven and groaned. He said to the deaf man, "Be opened."

All at once the man could hear. He could speak plainly, and people could understand him. Everyone was surprised. They said about Jesus, "He makes the deaf hear and those who can't speak talk."

❖   Ask Jesus to help you hear and say only good things.

The Soldier's Servant

Based on Matthew 8:5–13

A soldier who worked for another country once came up to Jesus. He begged, "Lord, my servant is at home in great pain. He can't even move."

Jesus said, "I will come and cure him."

The soldier answered, "Lord, you are too great to enter my house. Only say the words right here, and my servant will be healed. I know how powerful words can be. When I say, 'Do this' to a man who is under me, he does it."

Jesus was surprised at the man's faith in his power. He said that it was the greatest faith he had ever seen. Jesus told the soldier, "You may go. Let what you believed would happen be done for you."

At the same moment Jesus said these words, the soldier's servant became well.

❖ Tell Jesus how great he is for something he has done.

23

24

Bartimaeus,
the Blind Beggar

Based on Mark 10:46–52

Jesus, his friends, and a crowd of people were leaving the city of Jericho. Bartimaeus, a blind man, was sitting at the side of the road, begging. He heard all the noise and asked, "What's happening?"

People told him, "Jesus of Nazareth is passing by."

Bartimaeus started shouting, "Jesus, Son of David, have pity on me!" The people scolded Bartimaeus and told him to be quiet, but he called out even more loudly, "Son of David, have pity on me."

Jesus heard Bartimaeus and stopped. He said, "Bring the man to me."

The people said to Bartimaeus, "Have courage. Get up. Jesus is calling you." Bartimaeus threw off his cloak, jumped up, and went to Jesus.

Jesus asked Bartimaeus, "What do you want me to do for you?"
The blind man answered, "Lord, please let me see."
"Go," Jesus said. "Your faith has made you well."
Suddenly Bartimaeus could see. He followed Jesus down
the road, praising God.

❖   Praise Jesus for the power to see beautiful things, colors,
    and the faces of people who love you.

Lazarus Lives Again

Based on John 11:1–44

Jesus had three good friends in Bethany, Lazarus and his sisters, Mary and Martha. One day the sisters sent this message to Jesus: "Master, the one you love is sick." When Jesus heard this, he said, "This illness will be for God's glory." Jesus waited two days and then went to Bethany.

By the time Jesus came to Bethany, Lazarus had died. Martha went to meet Jesus. She said, "If you had been here, my brother would not have died."

Jesus said, "Your brother will rise. Whoever believes in me will never die."

Mary and other friends of the family came out to Jesus. They were crying. Jesus asked, "Where have you laid Lazarus?" Then he cried too.

They took Jesus to Lazarus's tomb. It was a cave with a stone in front of it. Jesus ordered, "Take away the stone." Martha said, "Lord, there will be a smell. He's been dead for four days."

Jesus said, "Remember, if you believe, you will see God's glory."

The men moved the stone. Jesus looked up to heaven and prayed, "Father, I thank you for hearing me." Then he called in a loud voice, "Lazarus, come out!" And Lazarus, wrapped in burial clothes, walked out of the tomb. Jesus said, "Untie him and let him go free."

❖ Thank Jesus for the gift of everlasting life.